ABOUT THE AUTHOR

Shane Jones was born in February of 1980. His poetry
and short fiction have appeared in numerous literary
journals, including *New York Tyrant*, *Unsaid*, *Typo* and
Pindeldyboz. He lives in upstate New York. This is his
first novel.

LIGHT
BOXES

Shane Jones

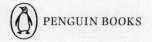 PENGUIN BOOKS

PENGUIN BOOKS

Published by the Penguin Group

Penguin Group (USA) Inc., 375 Hudson Street, New York, New York 10014, U.S.A.

Penguin Group (Canada), 90 Eglinton Avenue East, Suite 700, Toronto,
   Ontario, Canada M4P 2Y3 (a division of Pearson Penguin Canada Inc.)

Penguin Books Ltd, 80 Strand, London WC2R 0RL, England

Penguin Ireland, 25 St Stephen's Green, Dublin 2, Ireland (a division of
   Penguin Books Ltd)

Penguin Group (Australia), 250 Camberwell Road, Camberwell, Victoria 3124,
   Australia (a division of Pearson Australia Group Pty Ltd)

Penguin Books India Pvt Ltd, 11 Community Centre, Panchsheel Park,
   New Delhi - 110 017, India

Penguin Group (NZ), 67 Apollo Drive, Rosedale, North Shore 0632,
   New Zealand (a division of Pearson New Zealand Ltd)

Penguin Books (South Africa) (Pty) Ltd, 24 Sturdee Avenue, Rosebank,
   Johannesburg 2196, South Africa

Penguin Books Ltd, Registered Offices:
80 Strand, London WC2R 0RL, England

First published in the United States of America by Publishing Genius Press 2009
Published in Penguin Books 2010

10 9 8 7 6 5 4 3 2 1

PUBLISHER'S NOTE
This is a work of fiction. Names, characters, places, and incidents either are
the product of the author's imagination or are used fictitiously, and any
resemblance to actual persons, living or dead, business establishments,
events, or locales is entirely coincidental.

ISBN 978-0-14-311778-0
CIP data available

Printed in the United States of America
Set in Photina MT with New Century Schoolbook
Designed by Sabrina Bowers

For Melanie

The most serious charge which can be brought against New England is not Puritanism but February.

—Joseph Wood Krutch, *The Twelve Seasons*

LIGHT BOXES

Thaddeus

We sat on the hill.
We watched the flames
inside the balloons heat
the fabric to neon colors.
The children played
Prediction.

They pointed to empty holes in the sky and waited. Sometimes all the balloons lit up at once and produced the nightly umbrella effect over the town beneath, whose buildings were filling with the sadness of February.

Nights like this will soon die, Selah whispered in my ear.

Days became cooler, clouds thickened. We sat on the hill. We watched the flames inside the balloons heat the fabric to neon colors.

Nights like this will soon die, said Bianca. She ran from the woods, where she saw three children twisting the heads of owls.

Nights like this will soon die, said the butchers, marching down the hill.

We sat there for the last time to watch the balloons, the neon colors stitched in our minds.

Pigs shrieked, and windows shattered across the town. A snout, massive and pink, traced the side of a balloon in its arc. The fabric stretched around the dark nostrils and stopped just before tearing, and it stayed there.

Still the children stood in a line with their lanterns raised to watch the first snowfall of February cover the crop fields.

Selah lowered her head. Selah folded her hands in her lap. Selah looked at the backs of the children's heads and saw ice form knots in their hair.

We can only pray, whispered Selah.

I looked at Selah and remembered the dandelions stuck in her teeth. I thought of a burning sun, an iceberg melting in her folded hands.

They held hands. They formed

dozens of circles around their deflated, smoldering balloons. Balloons, silken globes in the colors magenta, grass green and sky blue, were mud-strewn, wet with holy water and burned black through the stitching.

Bianca said, I don't understand.

Thaddeus said, I don't either.

Is this February's doing, she said.

Maybe, said Thaddeus, who looked up at the sky.

A scroll of parchment was nailed to an oak tree, calling for the end of all things that could fly. Everyone in town gathered around to read it. Trumpets moaned from the woods. Birds dropped from branches. The priests walked through town swinging axes. Bianca clutched Thaddeus's leg, and he picked her up under the arms and told her to hold him like a baby tree around the neck, and Thaddeus ran.

Back outside their home, the balloons were spread out on the ground. Baskets hacked by axes. The priests dipped their lanterns into the fabric of the balloons.

Thaddeus, Selah and Bianca and others from town formed a circle by holding hands.

February, they repeated until it became a chant. Until they all imagined a little tree sprouting through the center of their burning balloon.

The priests walked down the

hill and into town where they stopped at the town school and the town library. They confiscated textbooks, tore out pages about birds, flying machines, Zeppelins, witches on brooms, balloons, kites, winged mythical creatures. They crumpled up paper airplanes the children had folded, and they dumped the pages into a burning pit in the woods.

The priests sank their rusty spiked shovels into the mound of dirt and refilled the hole. Some of the priests felt tears roll down their cheeks but didn't feel sadness. Others forced their minds to unravel the memory of wind. They nailed a second scroll of parchment to a second oak tree. It stated that all things possessing the ability to fly had been destroyed. It said that no one living in the town should speak of flight ever again.

It was signed, February.

Thaddeus, Bianca and Selah painted

balloons everywhere they could. They pulled up floor-boards and painted rows of balloons onto the dusty oak. Bianca drew tiny balloons on the bottoms of tea-cups. Behind the bathroom mirror, under the kitchen table and on the insides of cabinet doors, balloons appeared. And then Selah painted an intricate inter-twining of kites on Bianca's hands and wrists, the tails extending up her forearms and around her shoulders.

How long will February last, Bianca asked, stretch-ing her hands out to her mother, who was blowing on her arms.

I really have no idea, said Thaddeus, who watched the snow fall outside the kitchen window.

In the distance the snow formed into mountains on top of mountains.

Finished, her mother said. You will have to wear long sleeves from now on. But you'll never forget flight. You can wear beautiful dresses—that's what you can wear.

Bianca studied her arms. The kites were yellow with black tails. The color melted into her skin. A breeze blew over the fresh ink and through her hair.

Thaddeus

I kept a kite hidden in my workshop where the priests couldn't find it. I unfolded the kite from its dusty box and told Bianca she could fly it for a few minutes. I tried to see if the priests were in the woods but only saw owls sidestepping through the snow.

I said to try again after the kite failed to take off. A hand pushed the kite to the ground. She tried a few more times, and the kite slammed downward. I saw a cloud shaped like a hand. I thought of Bianca and her happiness like bricks in mud.

It's February, said Bianca.

I said, I'm sorry this didn't work out. We can try again.

What's the point, she said. It's the end of flight. It's February.

The point, I said, is to keep trying for the sake of trying.

That week we attempted to fly the kite each night. But what felt like a wind gust on my skin wasn't enough to carry the kite. I went into my workshop, grabbed some glass jars, and back outside I handed them to Bianca. I took the kite and ran as fast I could. I ran like a madman, my mouth open in a sad air-swallowing attempt, heard Bianca laughing in the distance, looked for the priests in the woods sharpening their axes, dreamed of Selah and Bianca holding hands with August, carried the kite at my shoulder until I let it go and felt it collapse on my back. I fell face-first on the ground, ate snow and mud, tore my knee open on a rock.

Back up the hill, Bianca swirled the glass jars through the air. The kites on her arms twitched.

Here, she said, handing me the jars with careful, kite-stringed fingers. They are full now. Maybe the Professor can figure out what is wrong with our sky. Maybe we can figure out February.

Bianca

When I was really little, my father came into my bedroom with a sheet of fabric he said would one day fly in the sky.

I'll show you, he said, sitting down on the edge of the bed, then sliding toward the middle, where I sat with my legs crossed.

Through my bedroom window, I watched a tree lose a branch under the weight of snow that had been falling for months. Before the branch hit the ground, a sheet of yellow fabric floated down over my eyes. It felt like silk and smelled of oil and stream water.

I heard the clank of metal, and then a hot flame near the back of my neck, and then the fabric lifted from my face, and it bloomed into a giant flower that touched the ceiling and grew toward the corners of my bedroom.

What does this feel like, my father said.

It's like being inside one of those globes the shopkeepers make in town, I said, now standing on the bed, fingertips reaching toward the flower. It feels wonderful. It feels like happiness.

It will be called, my father said, a balloon.

In the crop field, four people are found standing with their heads tilted back and arms frozen to their sides. Eyes closed, their mouths stretched open and filled with snow.

Thaddeus was buying apples when

he overheard the group of former balloonists known as the Solution.

How much can we put up with. How many days will this dreadful season extend itself. Our town is a place of no flight and all snow because of February.

There were five of them, tall and thin, wearing long brown coats and black top hats. They had thin plastic masks over their faces. Each mask was painted as a different-colored bird.

You, said one of the members, who grabbed Thaddeus's shoulder and turned him around.

Thaddeus faced the Solution, holding his basket of apples tight against his chest.

We're starting a rebellion, a war, said a yellow bird mask, against February and what it stands for.

A war, repeated Thaddeus.

Yes, a war, a war, a war, the Solution repeated.

An orange bird mask continued, We're sick of February, who we believe is responsible not only for a season of endless gray and snow but the end of flight.

A blue bird mask lurched forward and placed a square of parchment in Thaddeus's coat pocket. He knocked one of Thaddeus's apples out of the basket and into a pile of snow.

Remember us, said the Solution.

And they disbanded, walking, dreaming of flying, in separate directions.

Professor

At the entrance to our town stands the Peter statue. Peter initiated the bird migration. This led to the age of flight, which is a rare time of recorded joy for our town. The sky was a land of balloon travel, bird flight patterns and flying-machine experiments. The afternoons were hot, the evenings cool when we went to the top of the hill to watch the nightly umbrella effect. We walked barefoot through streams. The children exploded in piles of corduroy leaves. We named the changes in weather Spring, Summer, Fall and February.

Peter believed in the life of flight even when he was bound with twine to his balloon by the priests and sent to a deadly altitude. Peter believed that the month of February should be eliminated, that it was possible to move clouds with long poles and extend the seasons of Spring and Summer. He said it could be taken further, that utopia included a town that knew only June and July. He wrote on archived parchment that if February were allowed to expand, it would infest our moods and kidnap our children.

Thaddeus

The Solution came to my window last night. They had on their bird masks and black top hats. They wore a single brown scarf around their necks. I said I understood the need to rebel and protect our town against February. I reminded them of the tactics used last year.

Most important, they said, think of your daughter, Bianca.

I saw that some snow had gathered in a corner on the ceiling. I grabbed a broom to sweep it away.

When I turned back around, the Solution was walking away into the snowfall. It looked like they were skipping.

I closed my eyes. I imagined Selah and Bianca in a canoe so narrow they had to lie down with their arms folded on their stomachs, their heads at opposite ends, their toes touching. I dreamed two miniature suns. I set one each upon their foreheads. I dreamed a waterfall and a calm lake of my arms below to catch them.

Bianca

I know it was important to get up, but my body felt too heavy. My parents stood next to my bed and spoke slowly and moved slower. They said their bladders were being filled with lead and soon it would rise into their chests. My father smiled and ran in place, a tactic used against February last year, but I could see tears in his eyes, and then he stopped, shoulders slouched forward, head near his knees. Lead poured from his mouth.

My parents climbed into bed with me. The smell of mint made my stomach hurt. They held me and told me everything would be fine, that sadness would rise from our bones and evaporate in sunlight the way morning fog burned off the river in summer. My mother rubbed the kites on my hands and arms and told me to think of my lungs as balloons.

I just want to feel safe, I said.

Thaddeus

The Professor told us that to protect Bianca we should feed her mint leaves. In the rare warm months, we grew as much as we could, taking precious crop space to harvest huge bushels of mint we use in the nightly tea, bathwater and

SELAH'S MINT SOUP

> 8 cups chicken stock
> 2 cups mint leaves
> 3 large eggs
> ½ teaspoon salt
> ¼ teaspoon black pepper

At night Selah rubs mint leaves into my beard and pats my lips dry with mint leaves. I braid mint leaves into Selah's hair. I whisper into her ear, You are my sparrow. Through the night we check on Bianca. When Bianca awakes screaming against February, Selah picks her up and holds her and tells Bianca to think of cloudless skies, a moose letting her hang by one hand from his nose.

Caldor Clemens

Thaddeus Lowe! The guy who flies balloons. I spent my days collecting sap from the trees. Still do. Always covered in sap, tree bark splintered under my nails.

I'd be in the woods loosening the buckets and I'd hear the sky hissing. I'd look up. I'd see a scrawny guy with a beard in a basket that had a balloon fastened above it. The balloon was yellow with green stitching. He couldn't have been more than a few feet above the tallest tree. At one point the basket brushed the heads of the trees and pinecones rained down. Gave me a nasty gash on my nose. I tasted blood, but that was no bother.

I went up in a balloon once with my sisters and we watched the sun roll across the horizon, clouds going red and pink, colors swirling around us in a mist. I shouldn't be thinking about that anymore, because flight is over. Some people in this town say the more thoughts you have about flight the worse February haunts you. And then there's the priests, who have locked away believers of flight someplace at the edge of town. But that's just a dumb rumor. Could be true, though. If given the chance, I'd break open the skull of February. I'd swing a nice big bucket of sap right into the side of his head and watch the ice of his mind explode like confetti.

Last night everyone in town dreamed the clouds fell apart like wet paper in their hands.

Six Reports from the Priests

1. The Solution attempted to fly today.

2. They failed.

3. To hell with February, one member shouted. The rest cheered. They are a loud bunch. They wear bird masks. They throw apples through clouds.

4. The balloon collapsed on one side. The flames shot up. The flames spilled out and crawled across the field and up the birch trees, where flightless birds burned.

5. The snow continues to fall.

6. There has been talk of a war.

When Thaddeus arrived home

he told Selah about a war against February. She bathed Bianca in mint water, ran a cloth in circles around her back.

I don't know if a war will help anything, she said.

It's the Solution, said Thaddeus. They have nothing to lose. I don't know. It's something we should consider. For her sake. He tilted his head toward Bianca.

Come, said Selah, and Thaddeus followed her voice as if the word were a hook thrown from the bath-water.

He knelt down beside the tub and placed his face in the mint water. Bianca felt him close to her back. The water rose to her chin. She remembered what it was like to swim in the river with June. The drain in the tub was a fish biting her toe. Thaddeus held his face in the water long enough for the mint to be fully absorbed into his beard.

There, said Selah tugging upward with a fistful of Thaddeus's hair.

Water poured from his beard. Thaddeus walked into the kitchen and made a cup of tea, then went back into the bathroom. He watched his wife continue to bathe Bianca. He made sure to tip the teacup high enough when he sipped so that Bianca could see the balloon painted on the bottom.

Bianca whispers into the bathwater.

Maybe the priests aren't really priests. Look at the way their silly robes move.

I want to be safe. I want to live inside a turtle shell.

Thaddeus tugs on his beard.

A little mint water drips on his palm. He rubs his hands together. He walks into Bianca's bedroom and soothes her arms and legs with his hands. The idea is that any sadness that occurs during sleep can be decreased by infusing mint into the skin, into the lungs and heart. Thaddeus and Selah take turns, applying the mint throughout the night.

Before daybreak, Thaddeus smells honey and smoke coming from Bianca's bedroom.

In her room he notices that the window is open and snow is blowing in.

He throws the covers off the bed.

He looks around the room.

He looks under the bed.

He looks in the closet.

He looks in the hallway.

He looks at his feet.

He looks at the bed. He looks at the bed.

Bianca's bed is a mound of snow and teeth.

Bianca is gone.

Thaddeus

I've been spending more time alone on the hill. I can't remember it being colder than it is now. The ground is frozen and black, the town windows webbed in snow and ice. When I spark a fire from found branches a snowball falls from the sky and douses the flame. I look up at the sky, the gray waves rolling along. I am growing tired and sad at the disappearance of my daughter and it stirs deep inside me. I snap off a tree branch. I whirl it around in huge circles before letting it fly skyward.

It flies up, much higher than I imagined, and, climbing higher and higher, it rips through a cloud's leg, peaks in flight, then descends again, tearing another hole through the shoulder of a cloud.

In the first hole, there's a pair of feet dangling from the edge. In the second hole, there's a man walking around a dark room. I call down to the house for Selah who is shaking out Bianca's bedsheet, which disintegrates into a little blizzard.

Am I dreaming right now, I shout. Can you check the bed to see if I'm sleeping.

No, you're not dreaming, she yells back after going inside to check our bed. You're standing outside by yourself with your thoughts. Your daughter has been kidnapped and your thoughts are torturing you. Sometimes you wake in the middle of the night from terrible dreams, but right now you are awake.

I watch the two holes in the sky until a new breaking of gray rolls across.

My mind is ice.

Selah yells, I want our daughter back.

Deer run against the edge of the woods. Twisted through their antlers is a long quilt, a banner. The quilt says, WAR AGAINST FEBRUARY NOW WAR AGAINST FEBRUARY NOW WAR AGAINST FEBRUARY NOW. The Solution waves from under the pine trees. A man is collecting sap.

I hesitate but wave back.

Thaddeus to Bianca

I climb on the roof. Your bedroom is beneath me. I close one eye and reach my hand out and tear open the horizon. I pull the sky up and toward me like old wallpaper. I see you sleeping in a bed of duck feathers. I close both eyes and finish the dream of us in a balloon. The new sky smells like the ocean. It feels like crushed velvet when you push against it to send the balloon toward your mother waiting on the hill.

Questions

Thaddeus asks the children twisting the heads of owls if they have seen a small girl named Bianca in yellow pajamas. The three children sit against an oak tree with their legs stretched out, snow as a blanket to their waists.

Do the yellow pajamas have flowers printed at the hem, asks the middle child.

Yes, Thaddeus says.

Does the little girl have dark hair that smells of honey and smoke, asks the child to the left.

Thaddeus shakes his head. No, he thinks, she never smelled of honey and smoke. But the room did. Yes, the room.

The room smelled of honey and smoke. Bianca has dark hair. Her hair doesn't smell of honey and smoke, but the room did.

Does the little girl have a drawing of kites on her hands and arms, asks the child to the right.

Yes, says Thaddeus. Her mother painted those kites. Where is my daughter. What has happened to my daughter.

The children go back to concentrating on twisting the heads of the owls.

No, we haven't seen her, they say.

I don't understand, though, you said, Thaddeus

says. Now, if you don't mind, sir, we are much enjoying ourselves by playing with these owls. I hope you find the little girl. She sounds very cute and very beautiful.

For the rest of the day Thaddeus asks every person in town if they have seen his daughter. Everyone says no. The Solution walks past Thaddeus.

We could help, they say, smiling.

The one with the blue bird mask hands Thaddeus an apple, apologizes, then runs to catch up to the group.

Selah and Thaddeus don't sleep

for several days, in which they decide that a war against February is needed to cure their sadness. They invite the Solution to their home, who talk for hours on strategy to destroy February. When they drink their tea, they lift up their bird masks to expose their blue-wintered lips. Thaddeus tries not to cry when a yellow bird passes him a list of missing children and asks Thaddeus to please add Bianca's name where there is room. He reads the list over. His eyes fill with tears. He writes down Bianca's name.

Will a war bring my daughter back, asks Thaddeus.

The birds all look at one another.

It's possible, they say. Anything is possible when you start a war.

I want my daughter back, says Thaddeus. I want her back, and I want my wife to be safe.

He holds her hand.

The Catalog of Missing Children

Evie Rhodes—taken from her bed on February the 127th

Candace Smith—disappeared while feeding birds on February the 175th

Adam Johnston—vanished while playing in a closet on February the 112th

John Smith—also disappeared while feeding birds on February the 175th

Daniel Hill—considered lost in the woods on February the 212th

Joyce Aikey—drowned while diving for turtles on February the 188th

Joseph Mendler—taken from his bed on February the 139th

Estrella Roberts—vanished during a game of hide-and-seek on February the 144th

Emily Boyce—drowned during a snowball fight on February the 222nd

Sarah Lock—disappeared in a blizzard on February the 247th

Bianca Lowe—taken from her bed on February the 255th

Peter Tuner—never came home from school on February the 199th

Jessica Chambers—vanished while walking with her dogs on February the 312th

Suzy Peck—taken from her bed on February the 322nd

Caldor Clemens

I was Thad's number-one guy during the war against February. That's right, number one. The right-hand man. Top wolf. Or top dog. Whatever.

I thought Thad was crazed because of the kidnapping of Bianca. But after I noticed a change in the ways of the town during the season of February, I went to his house with the Solution to talk about the war. Each week we recruited more and more people from the town, a whole mess of us cramped up there. Everyone drank tea or some shit. I drank vodka with mud.

Before Thad spoke, the Solution told me he was the one they were looking for to lead the war. He was their guy. He was their wolf to lead this war. All right, I thought, let's see what this guy has got to say.

The one thing that really made me want to be a part of the war, besides the fact that it was bloody exciting, was what Thad and the Professor showed us one night. It was called a mood chart. It explained how our moods change by the seasons. Now, I'm not the Professor, but it was real clear that something was happening to us during the season of February. The sadness quotient peaked, or whatever it's actually called. Thad pointed to a chart with an ascending line and a frowning face. And to hear about his poor little girl missing and to see my own kids knocking their heads against a wall all February long, it made me so angry that I decided I would give my heart, my blood, for the War Effort.

The first attack on February

occurs. Thaddeus, Selah, Caldor Clemens and the Solution devise a plan to trick February by pretending it's summer. The men take their shirts off and roll their pants into a ring at their kneecaps and call them shorts. Selah wears a thin summer dress, the one she wore while on her first balloon trip with Thaddeus. It smells like cedar and grass clippings from the floor of his workshop. The rest of the women wear skirts. They unbutton their blouses and untie their bonnets.

The War Effort claps while discussing the warm weather. They imagine beams of unfiltered sunlight striking their backs as they tend to the crops.

Caldor Clemens pretends to pick berries. He wipes sweat from his brow before diving into a pile of snow and swimming.

Thaddeus and Selah move away from the group to make love in the naked snow. They tell each other to concentrate on the ocean teasing their toes, the sand in their hair. Selah imagines that the melting snow between her legs is sweat. Thaddeus licks the ice from her lashes, pushes into the snow. They feel watched and excited.

At the end of the day, the group struggles to smile. Their bones are frozen. They walk into Thaddeus and Selah's home to have tea. Everyone is exhausted, their faces beaten red by February.

We should continue with this tactic until we see some progress, says Thaddeus.

They all agree by way of tipping their teacups.

Selah

One of the strongest supporters of the war was a wild man named Caldor Clemens. Clemens was a former member of the group of balloonists known as the Solution. The Solution was a collective of nine or ten bird-masked men who refused to obey the laws of the end of flight. The Solution staged free falls off the tops of buildings and tied kites like leashes to shop doors. They were an aggressive bunch.

I wanted my daughter back. I wanted my husband to be safe. So when I saw Caldor Clemens, all seven feet, three hundred pounds of him standing at my door with tears running down his cheeks, I pulled him into my home by the wrist and told him that the blame could be placed directly on February. That a war can only help us.

This is Caldor Clemens, I said.

It's nice to meet you, said my husband.

Scraps of Parchment Found Under Selah's Pillow

I want my daughter back.
I want my daughter back.
I want my daughter back.
I want my daughter back.
I want my daughter back.
I want my daughter back.
I want my daughter back.

I want my daughter back.

I want my daughter back.
I want my daughter back.
I want my daughter back.
I want my daughter back.
I want my daughter back.
I want my daughter back.
I want my daughter back.
I want my daughter back.
I want my daughter back.
I want my daughter back.

I want my daughter back.

I want my daughter back.
I want my daughter back.

Thaddeus

Today I took a trip into town with Caldor Clemens. The air was cold and smelled like apples. I saw a fox sitting on a mailbox. He had duck feathers in his mouth. People asked about the war against February. We couldn't answer the questions fast enough. The crowd circled us ten rows deep.

Here, said Clemens, and he knelt down. Feeling somewhat foolish, I climbed onto his shoulders, where I sat perched high above the crowd once he stood.

I told the townsfolk that the war against February was as necessary as the air we breathed. If we refused to fight back, the cold and gray would settle like an endless blanket of rocks. I told them to remember what it was like to hold hands with May. I told them to remember what the streams sounded like outside their bedroom windows, the water pouring over August rocks, the birds calling from branches of green, dogs howling in the plains. I told them to close their eyes and ignore the snow melting on their faces but to remember what it looked and felt like when they woke in the morning to the sun draped over their beds, over their bare feet.

Clemens reached up and grabbed me around my ribs. He lifted me from his shoulders with a strange grace and elegance and placed me back on my own two feet.

Great speech, Thad. Really, really, really good.

Clemens punched me in the shoulder. It left a bruise the shape of a mallet's head.

Caldor Clemens

Thad paused for a moment. The smell of mint leaves rose like smoke from his skin. Then he mumbled a few positive comments. LIFE IS GOOD. PEOPLE LAUGH WITH JULY. FEBRUARY IS NOTHING, BECAUSE FEBRUARY IS SHIT. He didn't really say that last one. I said that. The smell stopped. He pointed at the sky. He told me to look for a girl's feet through a hole. He said they could be Bianca's. I didn't see anything but clouds suffocating little stars. We watched for a few minutes until he said that a man and a woman were in a second hole. Still I didn't see a damn thing. Thad said that the man and woman were fighting, throwing balls of paper at each other. I kept looking. Kind of crazy to think about holes in a sky. But maybe I did see two shadowy figures in that one hole. Who knows? I was drunk on cider, vodka and mud.

Orange Bird Mask

Today we go up the hill with our weather-changing poles. Some of them are fifty feet long, requiring a dozen men to raise them. The idea is to destroy the clouds that cover the sun. An old Peter tactic he never had the chance to try.

It fails, because when we raise the weather poles, an ice storm freezes them together. They blow down the hill and toward the town. One weather pole spikes a shopkeeper's window.

By nightfall we feel the sadness inside us that is February. I can smell the mint evaporating from Selah and Thaddeus.

Not every tactic will be effective against February, Thaddeus says. Everyone stay positive.

The War Effort has doubled since the great Thaddeus speech. We now have blacksmiths and sculptors and farmers and a little person and beekeepers, and most of them have lost their children to February. Most of them can't unclench the fingers-into-fists that are their hearts.

Go home and make a large fire, Thaddeus tells us. Warm yourself until your sweat soaks through your clothes.

Thaddeus

February has destroyed dozens of our limbs. Infected men stay in bed where they are sad and useless. The rest of us stay up at night sketching plans for a new war strategy. We take turns pacing, crumpling paper, disregarding each idea that springs from our cold mouths. Selah makes tea with two crossed mint leaves floating on the top of each cup. Without an idea, we question if we should even continue our daily assault of warm-weather tactics. A few of the men have dressed for the day in long pants and sweaters. They throw up their hands and walk out the door. Selah is standing in the doorway trying to make out the mountains behind the clouds. She drops her teacup. Then she says I should come look. I walk over, and she points to her feet and raises her finger up to the roofs of the town. The hot tea has burned a path through the snow from our front door and down into the town.

They find Bianca dead on

the riverbank. Two members of the War Effort drag her from the water and place her arms at her sides, rest her head on a rock. The members stare. She's covered in blue ink, random letters they can't form into words. When they tell Thaddeus, the smell of mint leaves is so strong it turns the windows in town green and the clouds look like moss.

Thaddeus tries to decipher the words, hopes for a complete sentence. He sends a messenger for the Professor.

The only word the Professor can make out is OWLS.

You should know that I would like to join the war against February, says the Professor.

Fine, says Thaddeus, buttoning his coat.

In a few days you should call a meeting. There is something you need to see, the Professor says. It's a tactic against February. I think it could help.

Very well, says Thaddeus. A meeting tomorrow at my home. Good-bye.

The Professor's plan for light

boxes was a mess of equations and diagrams nearly three hundred parchment sheets long. He didn't sleep for days, using Thaddeus's workshop to construct the first light box. When the pounding of metal, the sawing of wood, the breaking of glass, the tearing of paper stopped on the night of the fifth day, he emerged with his face covered in black grease and arms bloodied.

It's finished, he told Thaddeus. He picked glass from his knuckles with his teeth and spit them out. Let's begin the meeting so I can explain the effectiveness of light boxes.

The War Effort gathered. They watched the Professor lift the light box over his head and set it down until it was tight against his shoulders. In his right hand he held a dented metal box that had a cord attached. Lifting the metal box, he said in a muffled voice, Now, this is the power supply that when switched will simulate the light of the sun which we haven't seen in a year. The light box itself was constructed of wood fastened at odd angles with metal clamps, except for the front, which was a panel of glass. The top of the glass was where the light was going to shine—bulbs, the Professor called them. As he toggled the switch, everyone could see the sadness and frustration in his face, his eyes looking up at the bulbs as his head jerked from side to side. The switch clicked uselessly. He violently shook the metal box. He clutched the sides of his head and lost his balance a little.

Then the stench of burning leaves, and the bulbs bloomed crystal white across his face. The War Effort cheered. Some ran out into the snow-filled plains to mock the sky. Others took turns fitting the box over their heads, letting the light soak into their winter beards, their tongues tasting the blood from their splitting lips.

When Thaddeus went back into

the woods the three children weren't there. Thaddeus looked up and saw the owls on a branch. He asked them if they had seen the three children. Owls can't speak, and Thaddeus felt foolish. He walked around looking for footprints. A parchment was nailed to the tree. It stated that the three children had been kidnapped and should be added to the catalog of missing children. It was signed, February. Thaddeus saw footprints leading from the tree. They stretched several yards, then formed a circle. They continued straight, then another circle, then straight again. After each circle was a new type of footprint: bear, deer, squirrel, human, et cetera. The footprints continued this way as far into the woods as Thaddeus could see.

List Written by February and Carried in February's Corduroy Coat Pocket

1. I am not a bad person. I have enjoyed June, July and August like everyone else.

2. I fed you dandelions and picked the stems from your teeth with my tongue.

3. You smell of honey and smoke. That's what I call you. Girl who smells of honey and smoke. But you're more than that. You're a field of dandelions.

4. I have this nightmare where I'm standing in the field of dandelions holding a scythe. The horizon is children marching. Each child holds one of your teeth.

5. I'm so confused it almost feels calm.

6. I am guilty of kidnapping children. I am guilty of Bianca and causing great pain to Thaddeus and Selah and the town.

7. I want to be a good person, but I'm not.

Thaddeus

The first hot-water attack takes place from our home on the hill. We spend the first night filling large buckets with boiling water. We keep them hot by lighting small fires with piles of tree branches. We pour the buckets downhill toward the town. A cloud of steam rises into the sky as wide, empty trenches expand in the snow. The War Effort applauds like they are watching theater. The midget does somersaults down the hill. For a moment yellow streaks the sky. When I angle my face into the rays of sun, I notice the sky trembling around one of the holes. I see footprints running from the first to the second hole, where the dangling feet are no longer visible. I tell Selah to look up. She does but says she doesn't see anything except the clouds separating a little. And then the sky flutters like a flag, and then it goes black like closed curtains of wool.

Bianca

I could be in an underground cell. I could be dead. I miss air. I miss my father and mother. Every once in a while, the darkness disappears and I can see a man for a few minutes. Like yesterday when yellow streaked the room. He's tall with hips like mine. I believe this is February. He doesn't wash himself or clean his clothes. His hair is thick and uncombed, his beard scraggly, his pants torn, his shirt a faded gray. He sits at a desk or walks around the small room where he lives and where I stay hidden behind furniture. He cries a lot, too. Sometimes he just sits at his desk staring at the blank sheets of paper in front of him. But eventually he'll move and write something down and get up and walk around again. February drinks too much coffee. In the afternoon he eats food that's two thick slices of bread with a gooey substance and animal parts on the top. February is happy when he eats this meal. Sometimes the animal parts fall off the bread and onto the floor, but February doesn't mind. He just reaches down and picks them off the dusty wood floor and eats. One time I saw him staring out the window at the snow falling, and he started to cry really loud. There are two holes in the floor. Sometimes I sit on the edge of one. Sometimes I think of jumping down.

Thaddeus curled himself around the

backside of sleeping Selah. In a hazy voice she asked if they would know June again. Thaddeus closed his eyes and saw the town burn to the ground as he nodded his nose down the bumps of her spine. He opened his eyes. He thought of Bianca. When he fell asleep, he dreamed the clouds falling apart, the town starting anew. And when he woke in the morning he tried to remember the dream but couldn't, no matter how long he spent on the hill with his eyes shut.

Selah, he yelled down the hill toward their home. Do you remember the dream I had last night.

Selah was pouring buckets of hot water around their home. She yelled back that she didn't remember, but it was probably about balloons.

Of course, said Thaddeus. I would dream about balloons and flight. Thank you.

Selah wished for a moat to protect their home from February. Selah wished for the end of February and endless sadness and the end to missing children. Selah wished for the rebirth of town and flight. Selah wished for a scrap of something beautiful.

Thaddeus

After three days of dumping hot water by single buckets, our arms are long bruises unable to handle the turning of the sparrow-head faucet. Caldor Clemens invents the water-trough–horse system. He works for two days hacking down oak trees and carving out the trunks with knives and axes. When he finishes, the wooden trough is three times longer than our home. It stretches to the middle of where the cornfields used to grow. Clemens shows us how to stick bits of glass to the bottom of the trough with birch sap he has collected in buckets. The trough itself won't catch fire this way, he says, and lights a small fire beneath it. The water simmers. Clemens brings six horses up the hill and harnesses them with leather straps to the trough he has readied with boiling water. He raises his hand and sticks the fingers of the other in his mouth and whistles louder than I have ever heard a man whistle. The horses bolt forward, sending a wave of water rushing toward the town, melting the snow into slush.

We continue the attack for the rest of the week, until the streets clear—we want unfrozen land—and the snowfall melts on the soil like a massive tongue. The children say the clouds look like rippling sails. The holes in the sky turn pink and a body falls from the sky and into the river. The War Effort, their fingers sticky with sap, point to the sky shouting for the death of February.

FEBRUARY SAT ON A COTTAGE FLOOR
with a girl who smelled of smoke and
honey. The girl was telling him that she
was tired of being around someone who
carried so much sadness in his body.
February drew his kneecaps to his eye
sockets.

February apologized. He rocked back
and forth. When he stretched his legs back
out the girl was smiling and running in
place. February asked what she was doing.
The girl who smelled of honey and smoke
said it was to cheer him up.

I don't think that's going to work, said
February. I'm sorry, but it just won't.

Just try it, said the girl who smelled of
honey and smoke. Please.

February stood up and ran in place. His
joints popped. He bumped into a table,
knocking over a jug of water.

Looks like a flood, said the girl who
smelled of honey and smoke, who pumped
her legs and arms faster.

It does, said February, who watched the
water expand across the table and drip
onto the floor with great delight.

War Member Six
(Green Bird Mask)

The hot water worked better than we imagined. There was some flooding on account of the melted snow, but we used most of it to refill the buckets. February is breaking apart at the horizon seams. There are few clouds. The sky is a soft blue. The children's cheeks are flushed red from the sun.

People in town laughed today. Someone even skipped. The first sprouts of green crops can be seen on the hillside. The town feels alive and productive again.

We have won an early battle against February but know that anything can happen. For instance, there have been reports from the messengers that dark clouds are cascading from the mountain peaks. Grizzly bears were seen buttoning deer-skinned coats in case of freezing temperatures. The carpenters have boarded up their windows and refuse to leave their homes. They mumble sadness. Sadness sounds like bubbles blowing slowly in stream water.

THE GIRL WHO SMELLED OF HONEY

and smoke enjoyed collecting old books on plants. One night while out on the cottage porch sitting on the swinging bench with February, she opened to a chapter about vines and moss. One page had twelve different pictures of skinny green vines climbing the side of a Victorian brick house.

When the girl stood up to go inside and check on the pot roast she kissed February on his forehead. February flipped through the plant book until he stopped at a picture that showed a deer skeleton in a forest, spores of moss covering the white bone.

In only a week, the caption read, this deer skeleton will be blanketed with a spongy green moss.

The girl came back outside. She asked if he found anything interesting. She said the pot roast was ready. February nodded. He said that he liked the idea of moss.

Thaddeus

Spores of moss appeared on the horses' feet, and layers of green grew on their legs and backs. Selah spent her nights trying to defend against the attack of moss by pulling it out in patches and then soothing the horses' bloody flesh with wet magnolia petals. We continued the water-trough attacks until the moss collapsed each horse. A dark green blanket grew over their eyes.

Selah couldn't destroy the moss with her hands anymore, because it was so thick. It was now bigger than each horse. She slept next to the dying horses until the moss made its way down their throats. After the horses died, the moss moved its way from the woods and up the hill toward our home. Caldor Clemens swung the scythe like he was chopping wheat from an advancing crop field. He screamed and swore against February. Two priests came to sprinkle holy water around our home. They looked confused. The sky turned green, then black, then green again. A wolf stood on its hind legs and ripped opened its stomach. Ants carrying cubes of moss crawled out.

Eventually we tired. Clemens and I and the War Effort moved inside my home and barricaded the door with our backs. Then the moss moved its way under the door and over our boots.

Short List Found in February's Back Pocket

1. I've done everything I can.

2. I need to know you won't leave.

3. I wrote a story to show love, and it turned to war. How awful.

4. I twisted myself around stars and poked the moon where the moon couldn't reach.

5. I'm the kind of person who kidnaps children and takes flight.

Selah

To watch the way those horses died. To have felt the waves of their muscles contracting and shaking under that skin of mushy green. It was too much for me. The floor and walls and ceiling of our home were covered in moss. The dog was covered in moss but was still alive, and he ran around the home barking green-colored clouds. Thaddeus was tearing it out in fistfuls from the walls. Caldor was swinging a scythe in wide, low arcs.

Selah, said Thaddeus, start on the floor. Tear out what you can and burn it in the stove.

Caldor yelled at me as I stood there with my arms frozen to my sides. I thought about the way the horses died. I thought of death and war and the sadness of this once-colorful town.

Selah, please, the floor, said Thaddeus, who kicked his feet, flicked at the moss that grew over the toes of his boots.

I went back to where the horses were.

I knelt down in the cold, snow-freckled green. I peeled the moss away from their bodies. Their eyes had burst and their tongues were hanging out. Their necks were ropes of muscle and wet moss from the snow that now looked like green foam.

I placed my head inside a horse's neck. Deep inside

that web of flesh, among the organs and bone, I saw a miniature town that was identical to ours. I saw Thaddeus and Caldor and Bianca and everyone else asleep in hammocks tied to the ribcage. I saw a little balloon carrying horses in a basket. I saw kites pushing clouds into a burning sun. And where the stomach was, I saw myself standing on a frozen river. Wind tunnels around my legs lifted my dress and pulled my hair toward the clouds. I could feel the cracking of ice against the bottom of my feet. Fish ate water and screamed for me to come down and have some tea, have some mint.

Thaddeus

The shopkeepers in town said they saw Selah out on the river. One of them went after her. He reached his hand out, but she shook and stamped her feet. She broke the ice beneath her and fell.

I tried to save her, Thaddeus, said the shopkeeper, who was a little old man with a crooked back. He walked with a cane that had a curved end in the shape of an eagle, which he clutched.

I lay out on the ice as best I could and tried to find her through the hole. I'm sorry, sir, but what I saw, I don't know if it's February getting to me or not. But here, this is what I saw. He quivered, then straightened his back.

He handed me parchment paper. He shouted for the death of February, and a few other shopkeepers rallied around him, and they disappeared inside the inn. Outside the inn were great big heaps of wilting moss, dying ants, a butcher skinning a wolf.

I unfolded the parchment. I thought of Bianca and Selah and this ongoing war. I sat on the ground in the street as the wagons passed me by, the wheels slipping in the snow. There was a drawing on the parchment. It was drawn in lead and showed a woman, Selah, underwater. Brown fish with horse heads encircled her. Her hands were angry clouds. Kite strings were wrapped around her body, and she was screaming with a mouth full of snow.

It continued snowing and the

War Effort gathered around Thaddeus, who wouldn't move from the street. The shopkeepers cleared the snow around him with shovels. Thaddeus held a crumpled ball of parchment in his fist and refused to speak. At one point a wagon wheel crushed his hand, but he didn't flinch.

There's still a war to fight, one War Effort member said.

The town needs you, said another.

Caldor Clemens grabbed Thaddeus by the shoulders and shook him.

You can place your frustration on February, he said, looking into the dark eyes of Thaddeus.

Thaddeus mumbled and tightened his fists but didn't move. Three war members—blue bird mask, a carpenter and Caldor Clemens—tried to push him over. Caldor said that it was like trying to move a chimney. They had no choice but to leave him in the street night after night after night.

The left side of my body is Bianca, and my right side is Selah. With no body I have no reason to move from this spot.

I dreamed you a field of running horses, Selah. For you, Bianca, a balloon the size of the sky, my body a kite you can throw into the air.

Pull me by string and horse.

Tell me everything won't end in death. That everything doesn't end with February. Dead wildflowers wrapped around a crying baby's throat.

I've slowed my heartbeat to three beats a minute. I've redrawn the clouds into birds, a fox chasing them into the mountains.

I'm going to move my hand today.

I vomit ice cubes.

There's a ghost next to me.

Get up, Dad.

FEBRUARY WATCHES THE SNOWFALL.
He thinks about the senseless deaths of
Selah and Bianca and the ongoing war
against him. He creates ten different
shades of gray in the sky and then starts
over again. The girl who smells of honey
and smoke calls for him to come inside. He
thinks, She has a light in her throat when
she speaks. She has strings of light draped
inside her body.

There's a terrible war against me, he
says over his shoulder.

I know, she says. You can stop it anytime
you want.

The girl who smells of honey and smoke
can't hear him cry but can see the curled
shoulders. She can see his black shake.

Sculptor

Bianca's ghost appears in town. She wears red shorts and a white blouse and has long black hair. I watch her buy mint leaves and talk to shop owners about how soon until we will only experience summer. She walks through the streets passing out tulips whose petals have veins that spell out the word July. A barkeep tells everyone that Bianca's ghost has a War Plan involving the town children who have been kidnapped by February. An apprentice of mine says that when Bianca cupped her hands together it showed an entire sky of kites.

Thaddeus hadn't spoken in a week. But when Bianca's ghost whispered in his ear, he stood up. He pointed at the sky. He went to his home, where Caldor Clemens had taken over the War Effort. Bianca's ghost disappeared into the woods.

Since Thaddeus's solitude it's never been so cold or dark in the town. My owl statues became brittle with frost and cracked and crumbled to dust, and I'm lucky I haven't any children left to feed. That's a horrible thing to say, but it's true.

OWL STATUES——HALF PRICE.

Caldor Clemens gave a shirtless

speech under the two holes in the sky. The War Effort sat in a circle around Clemens, who pumped his fists and spit into snowbanks.

Thaddeus came up the hill carrying a scythe over his shoulder. He swung it across the snow tops, causing the War Effort to cheer and Clemens to tilt his head back and shout insults at the sky.

I'd like to add something, said Thaddeus, who moved into the center of the group and, in a gesture of respect to Clemens, took off his shirt.

As the snow fell on his skin, Thaddeus thought it didn't feel like snow. He prepared his mind to feel snow on skin. But that isn't what he felt, because the snow was torn parchment with letters scribbled in lead. In a fury Thaddeus collected the pieces of parchment from his shoulders and arms and every scrap from the hairy back of Clemens. The War Effort helped, too. They crawled on their hands and knees and gathered the parchment into a small pile.

Thaddeus and the Professor spent

the next week deciphering the fallen parchment. They sat at a wooden table in Thaddeus's kitchen where they could move the letters around. They took turns wearing the light box. War members brought them mint tea and tended to the fire.

There were over two hundred pieces of torn parchment. The Professor smacked the side of the light box, and the light flickered inside as they shuffled the letters.

What about this, said Thaddeus, and he moved the letters into a long row that stretched the length of the table.

FIND FEBRUARY AT THE EDGE OF THE TOWN
WEARING DARK CLOTHES FOLLOW ANIMAL
HUMAN FOOTPRINTS CREATED BY FEBRUARY AT
THE EDGE OF THE TOWN.

But it could be wrong, said the Professor. Look.

THE TOWN CREATED DARK FOOTPRINTS AT
THE EDGE OF ANIMAL CLOTHES.

HUMAN FOOTPRINTS WEARING DARK CLOTHES
AT THE EDGE OF THE TOWN.

See all the fruit, said Thaddeus.

Fruit, asked the Professor.

Yes, fruit, Thaddeus said, and spelled out more names of fruit grown during warm months.

The Professor continued moving the letters around. At the Edge of the Town appeared dozens of times.

And then the Professor began moving the pieces again and came up with something entirely different. He handed the light box to Thaddeus. He rubbed his face. Thaddeus said that At the Edge of the Town was where he should go. He told the Professor about the scroll of parchment left on the tree where three children once sat twisting the heads of owls. He told him about the tracks in the snow leading from the oak tree, the concentric circles, the animal prints, the human prints that might lead to February.

Very well, then, said the Professor. At the edge of the town.

If not, we'll go back to moving the parchment, and we'll find another answer, said Thaddeus.

Very well indeed, said the Professor. He put the light box back on.

72 |

List Found in February's Cottage Detailing Possible Cures for February

1. Valerian root and vitamin C tablets taken in the dark.

2. Yoga and meditation.

3. The melting of snow in children's palms.

4. Light boxes?

5. Hot bath taken with mint extract.

6. Touching the moon in places the moon doesn't know exist.

7. Consumption of St. John's wort.

8. Feeding the garden inside.

9. Giving Bianca back.

10. Twisting your fears into desires.

11. Mood diary.

12. Hydrating the body.

13. Paying attention to the girl who smells of honey and smoke.

Thaddeus tied a wool scarf

around his neck, looked at the picture the old man had given him of Selah and left home. Tree branches bowed with snow, their tips tied to the ground by invisible ropes. Thaddeus imagined standing behind February, running his knife in a half moon from ear to ear. He saw the blood wash the ropes away and the snow shake from the tress and the sky click to blue.

As Thaddeus walked through town, a few shopkeepers shook his hand. A butcher gave him a pork loin wrapped in twine. The old man appeared again, hobbled up to Thaddeus and handed him another folded parchment. Thaddeus unfolded it carefully. It showed himself standing behind a bearded man, running his knife around the man's throat.

Why would you draw this, asked Thaddeus.

But the old man was gone. Thaddeus thought through the yellowing candle at the inn window he saw him drinking from a beer stein. He thought the beer stein was decorated with balloons.

FEBRUARY WAS KIDNAPPING THE
children and burying them at the edge of
town. Anytime he looked into the town and
felt sadness he sent a group of priests
armed with shovels to dig a new hole.
What February didn't know was that not
all the children were dead. Some were
learning to survive underground, had built
an elaborate series of underground
tunnels. Someone was helping them. They
snuck out at night and gathered firewood
and stole lanterns. February couldn't see
what the children were planning
underground. He couldn't see their cold
faces illuminated in the fire and lantern
light, and he couldn't hear them discussing
the war against him. The children
dreamed the same dream the War Effort in
town dreamed. Flocks of birds tearing
through a new blue sky. They dug tunnels
that snaked beneath the town and placed
notes inside homes informing the people of
their own War Movement. Some children
weren't so lucky. February would watch
their fingers break a crust of snow, twitch
a little, and then seize in the wind as the
wolves moved in. It pleased February when
that happened. He went HAHAHAHAHA

and felt guilty for doing so. On more than one occasion, February looked under a roof for a child to kidnap and would see people wrapped in wool blankets and scarves and sweaters standing in a tight circle.

He would watch them undress after they unfolded parchment with words he couldn't make out.

FEBRUARY TRIED TO UNDERSTAND
the town. The girl who smelled of honey
and smoke told him he should drink more
tea with mint leaves. She placed her hand
around his bicep. Her thumb and pointer
finger touched. February looked back on
the town and saw the War Effort resume
the water-trough attacks. He saw
Thaddeus Lowe, and he saw the butcher's
knife hidden inside his coat pocket.

It wasn't my choice to do terrible things
to this town, said February to the girl who
smelled of honey and smoke. I didn't want
this to happen.

I pray each night for it to stop, said the
girl who smelled of honey and smoke. I've
had dreams of a woman helping us.
Thaddeus Lowe is coming with a knife,
said February.

Thaddeus Lowe is coming to kill me.

Maybe I can help, said the girl who
smelled of honey and smoke. It's the dream
I've had and what the woman has told me
to do.

I don't want to die, said February.

This is what is going to happen, said the
girl who smelled of honey and smoke. She

walked over to February and whispered something in his ear.

I hope that works, said February. I really do.

I'd do it for you. I'd change our entire story if I could, she said.

Our story, said February, is all wrong.

Back in town the blacksmiths

and carpenters are building a steel ship large enough to carry the population of the town. Caldor asks why build a ship and a blacksmith laughs and slams two iron planks against a dimpled metal block.

What do you think is going to happen when all this snow melts, the blacksmith says.

The blacksmith turns to a group of workers who are above him, constructing what will become the bow.

Is it too ridiculous to think we can sail away on the rivers that will flood our town. That we could end up in a New Town.

The blacksmiths raise their glowing tips of metal and shout no. Caldor tells one of the blacksmiths that Thaddeus Lowe will save them. The blacksmith laughs.

Thaddeus Lowe is an idiot, says the blacksmith. A fool.

Come here, says Caldor.

The blacksmith is about the same size as Caldor. Caldor spits in his face and simultaneously a bucket of frozen tree sap crashes into the side of the blacksmith's skull.

Caldor dangles the bucket over the body of the blacksmith.

Thaddeus Lowe is going to save this town, he says.

Caldor walks to where he can see the beekeepers

standing on the hill. From this distance, he thinks, the bees look like plumes of smoke around their hooded heads.

Beekeeper

One possibility is to attack with bees, I said. I could send thousands. The stings would force February to peel the clouds away. It's an idea. It could work.

I told this to Caldor Clemens while we sat in a balloon basket staring up at the sky, under where the two holes were rumored to be. The balloon itself rippled, was deflated around us on the snowy plains like a gown.

Go ahead and send them, Clemens said. Thaddeus would try it.

I tapped my head. A swarm of bees moved up my neck and formed a funnel extending skyward. The bees disappeared through the clouds, and there was a terrible buzzing sound. Then, seconds later, the funnel collapsed and thousands of my dead bees rained from the sky and filled the basket. Their little bodies were hard and cold. Clemens stood there staring at me while I shielded myself from the falling, dying bees.

The sadness was overwhelming.

What the shit, said Clemens, shifting his legs out of the dead-bee basket.

I watched him walk back into town, swatting dead bees from the nape of his neck.

That night Caldor Clemens had

a dream in which Thaddeus stood in a field with three owls. February was on his knees. The owls nodded the way owls nod. Thaddeus had his knife drawn.

I'm sorry for your daughter and your wife, but— you have the wrong guy, said February.

I don't care what you have to say. I only care about what you've done, said Thaddeus.

I can't help it. Really, I can't, February said.

I'm going to open your throat and fill you with tulips, Thaddeus said, grabbing February by the shoulder.

Wait, said February, there is someone I want you to meet first.

Running from the horizon and down the plains was a girl who smelled of honey and smoke.

Let me introduce you to my wife, said February.

List of Artists Who Created Fantasy Worlds to Try and Cure Bouts of Sadness

1. Italo Calvino

2. Gabriel García Márquez

3. Jim Henson and Jorge Luis Borges—Labyrinths

4. The creator of MySpace

5. Richard Brautigan

6. J. K. Rowling

7. The inventor of the children's toy Lite-Brite

8. Ann Sexton

9. David Foster Wallace

10. Gauguin and the Caribbean

11. Charles Schulz

12. Liam Rector

Like every other house in

town, Caldor Clemens's received a folded square of parchment from a group of children who came up from underneath his floor. There were dozens of them down there leaning against the sides of the tunnel. They raised their lanterns for the smallest to climb up over them and hand Clemens the parchment paper.

Is Bianca Lowe down there, said Clemens.

Who is Bianca Lowe, the smallest child said.

Bianca Lowe, said Clemens. Are you stupid. Sorry. I didn't mean that. She is a little girl with kites painted on her hands and arms. Her body was found on the riverbank. Sometimes her ghost walks around. I believe she may still be alive, since all of you seem to be. Clemens rocked from side to side. He tried to recognize a face.

The smallest child carefully turned around and asked the other children if they had seen a Bianca Lowe. A child at the bottom of the tunnel checked a scroll of parchment and called back that no such child was listed.

Here, said the smallest child, take this.

The square of parchment fit in the center of Clemens's palm like a pebble. It was tied with blue ribbon. On the blue ribbon in tiny gold letters it read, FINAL WAR PLAN AGAINST FEBRUARY.

Thank you, said Clemens. When he looked back down the tunnel, all the children were sliding into the flickering darkness swallowed up by lantern light.

FEBRUARY WAS SO WORRIED ABOUT
Thaddeus he didn't see the people in town
open their squares of parchment and read
the final War Plan against him. Some
people danced. Others cried. The War Plan
spread through the town and into the
trees, where the birds flapped their wings
and thought they could fly again. The
priests huddled, shook their heads and
waited for an order from their Creator.

Caldor Clemens was one of the people
who cried. Caldor told the members of the
War Effort that he would leave early the
next morning to find Thaddeus. After they
began the first steps of the children's War
Plan, they would follow Caldor's path of
dead bees through the woods. Then they
would all meet and head back into town,
together.

But when do we ready the balloon, said
one of the members of the War Effort, this
particular man an original member of the
Solution, who wore a purple bird mask.

I wasn't aware of a balloon, said
Clemens.

So you don't have a drawing of a balloon
flying in the sky on your parchment paper.

No, said Clemens. I don't.

Clemens studied all the parchment the War Effort had collected. Each was the same except for one that showed a balloon flying in the air. The parchment smelled of honey and smoke.

I don't know, said Clemens. Maybe that's the future or some shit.

Bianca

People in town think I'm a ghost, but I'm not. Even when I scream out: I'M NOT A GHOST I'M A REAL LIFE LITTLE GIRL WHO ISN'T DEAD. And: I JUMPED FROM A HOLE IN THE SKY WHERE FEBRUARY LIVES, the townsfolk still ignore the real me. They eat apples and clear the snow from the wagon wheels with iron bars. Things like, The smell of mint water filled the air, are said about me when I come around. Things like, Bianca's ghost began appearing in town, are written. Even my father thinks I'm a ghost. Do you think I'm a ghost. No, you don't think I'm a ghost. You're one of the good ones. You are kind and compassionate and filled with happiness. You walk through the season of February without a care in the world, maybe a shiver, only a passing complaint about the grayness of the sky that will soon give way to the flowers you planted around the mailbox.

Thaddeus

I came to a clearing where it was colder than any-
where else. There was a pile of chopped firewood and a
small log cabin that had moss growth on the door and
windows. I took out the knife the blacksmiths had
given me. I slowly approached the front door. The wind
blew at an incredible speed and the holes in my scarf
made my neck blister. I reminded myself of all the terrible things February had done to me and the town. I
calculated in my head that it was the 859th day of
February, and enough is enough, and God save me I
will slit the throat of February if it leads to warmer
seasons.

At the front door, I felt a wave of heat enter my body.
I smelled honey and smoke. I thought of Bianca and
her empty bedroom, the mound of snow with teeth. I
heard a woman's voice. I waited to hear the voice of
February. I imagined the depth of his voice, the endless
dark, lush layers.

Thaddeus, come in from out there, it's freezing, said
the woman's voice through the door. Don't you know
it's the middle of February. I have a pot of tea on the
stove and a fire going. It's like June 17th in here.

In the distance I heard wolves and saw priests running behind birch trees, and I think I heard the War
Scream of Caldor Clemens. I lost control of myself. I

took my shirt off and pulled my pants down. I let my entire body collapse against the front door, letting the warmth settle into my bones, the moss scratch at my eyes.

Bianca

Years ago when we experienced the season known as spring, my father woke me late in the night to show me the sun. He carried me to the top of the hill and told me to look toward the horizon where the pine trees stood. My father wiped the snow from my lashes, and there it was, a little marble of light behind the treetops.

That's the sun, my father said, and with any luck it will melt this snow so we can have summer.

I imagined that the birds flew and carried a lantern and placed it there in the treetops, because that's exactly what it looked like to me.

It looks like a lantern, I said.

My father smiled, then kissed me on the forehead. He promised it wouldn't be far away like that forever but would grow massive in the sky and warm my face.

Will it really do that.

Yes, Bianca, really, he said.

After seeing the sun, he carried me home and tucked me back in my bed and told me to sleep. But I couldn't. I spent the rest of the night and morning staring out the window, trying to see the lantern in the treetops carried there by birds. What everyone else called the sun.

War Effort Member
Number One
(Blue Bird Mask)

Caldor Clemens was hanged by his neck inside a hollow oak tree. His flesh had been torn open, and birds had made nests inside his stomach, chest, and neck. Other animals—bears, deer, a fox—had also been hanged, draped from tree branches by neon-blue string coiled around their necks. The mouth of Clemens had been ripped open. His bottom lip was at his chin and his top lip where his hair started. His mouth was filled with snow. A few teeth poked through.

We found the body of Caldor Clemens shortly after following him into the woods. We had completed the first steps of the children's War Plan, which was to put piles of dry brush throughout the town, and then we followed the trail of dead bees, just as Caldor had instructed. The War Effort has survived floods and moss and endless snowfall culminating in endless sadness. But the death of Clemens twisted our hearts in a different direction.

We found the spot where his body was, the tall, skinny trees bent in the middle and the ground rippled—the way I remembered waves looked breaking on the shore. War Effort Member Number Seventeen gripped my hand. The other members scanned the sky for two holes. When we came upon the death scene, two War Effort members sped off in opposite directions. Those who remained started to jog, smiling and complimenting each other.

Thaddeus

I opened the door to February's house and saw a girl with long black hair sitting at a desk. She was smiling and said, Please come in and take a seat. I declined. I asked her where February was. She said he had gone out to collect firewood and berries. The inside of the home was furnished in a way I had never seen before. Lamps and tables and chairs designed from another world. I noticed a fire burning low against the wall and columns of worn books stacked to the ceiling.

Who are you, I said.

I'm his wife, she said.

February has taken my wife and daughter and is destroying the town, I said.

I'm sorry. We, too, feel an overwhelming sadness. We, too, cry more than we laugh.

The girl stood up and walked over to me at the front door. She smelled of honey and smoke and when she got close enough images of cornstalks and birds and muddy salamanders crawled from my eyes. I felt dizzy. I grabbed her shoulders so I wouldn't fall. My body boiled to a blistering heat. Sweat poured out of me like lead.

There, there, Thaddeus, she said, embracing me with arms that reminded me of Selah. Don't worry about February. You can't control February.

My legs turned to mud. My knees hit the ground. My arms were around her waist now. Honey and smoke, honey and smoke, honey and smoke . . .

It was blurry. Then everything went black.

When I woke, I was sweating. I was sitting on the floor near the front door and the girl who smelled of honey and smoke was sitting at the desk, writing something on parchment paper.

Oh, you shouldn't see me writing this, she said. Just pretend you didn't see me writing this.

As I started to leave, I heard a man's voice and turned around to see, but it was only the girl who smelled of honey and smoke waving from the desk. When I stepped outside I took a deep breath and my lungs filled with warm air. The soil was soft and worms twitched in puddles. Birds flew from branch to branch. Flowers were sprouting up around the oak trees where squirrels fed. The sound of owls was so deafening you'd think something was wrong.

War Effort Member Number Two (Missing His Bird Mask)

Thaddeus was walking in our direction, waving his arms, whistling. A yellow bird mask next to me commented that Thaddeus was wearing a shirt without sleeves and pants torn at the knees.

A tactic against February, I reminded him.

We have lost the tips of our fingers and our toes are black inside our boots. Our beards are brittle with ice, our skin hard and red and cold.

He's going to freeze to death, said the War Effort member.

When we came upon Thaddeus, he laughed and gave each of us a great big embrace, patting us on the backs and kissing our faces. His arms had black spots where February had attacked, and his legs had ice for skin. When he placed his arms around me he felt like a thousand pounds.

Victory is ours, he said.

You killed February, we asked.

No, said Thaddeus. But look around. I didn't look around. I didn't need to. I didn't have to see the trees burdened with snow, the skies stuffed gray. Instead

I stared at Thaddeus as the snow fell on his bare arms.

What, said Thaddeus. Why is everyone looking at me like that.

War Effort Member
Number Three
(Purple Bird Mask)

Thaddeus talked of spring like it was blossoming around him. Where we saw snow and felt cold air, he saw crop fields and shielded his eyes from the sun with his hand.

Here, I said, handing Thaddeus a stack of papers detailing the children's war against February.

He read each page. He told us that if he had known that children were living underground with this kind of War Plan, February would have ended on the tenth day. Thaddeus then threw the papers into a pile of snow left yellow from a war member.

Call it off, he said.

The war members looked at each other until I retrieved the parchment papers and tried explaining to Thaddeus that February was still continuing, that the last week had been the worst yet.

Complete nonsense, said Thaddeus. We should get back to town and begin the spring harvest. Tell the underground children to come up and be children.

One War Effort member whispered into another's ear until it circled to the end, where I stood and heard,

Go to the Professor for help. I nodded back around the circle to each member. We nodded. Thaddeus laughed.

The Professor's Report on Thaddeus Lowe

Thaddeus Lowe believes that the current season is spring. On more than one occasion, he left my home to pick vegetables, which he pretended to cook over the fire I normally use to boil potatoes. To see this behavior from Thaddeus breaks my heart and I can only conclude that this is the cruelest of tricks from February.

Thaddeus laughed uncontrollably when I put the light box on. He slapped it off my head, knocking me from my chair and onto the floor.

Thaddeus asked several times why I was wearing a sweater and scarf.

Thaddeus laughed and shook his head each time I explained to him that it was February, that it had been February for nearly nine hundred days.

Thaddeus doesn't know who I am. He is oblivious to his surroundings.

I believe he has been poisoned, or spelled, or hypnotized by someone. It is difficult for me even to write this, for at this moment Thaddeus is standing outside without a shirt, commenting on the sun. In fact, it is a blizzard.

Thaddeus asked me twice if the children's war has

been called off. I told him that yes, I believe it has been.

I also told him about my rearranging of the paper that fell from the sky, but he cartwheeled away in the snow.

Bianca

The only people I was able to convince that I wasn't a ghost were the underground children. When I told them that the body found near the river was a fake, they said they already knew that. They said they knew the many tricks of February.

The children had developed an intricate maze of tunnels beneath the town, illuminated by hanging lanterns. At each junction there were little wooden signs with an arrow pointing up that said what part of town, what store, or what house was directly above you. I found my home and climbed up and shifted a floorboard to one side. My father was there talking about flying a balloon again. He was having an entire conversation with himself about how sweet the air tasted at a specific height. He described wind gusts by waving his arms through the air from side to side. He described the balloon ascending into the sky by stretching his arms to the ceiling and making a noise with his lips that sounded like the flame.

Before I went back down into the tunnel, the floorboard I had shifted to one side made a creaking noise. My father looked. He ran to me. He said I shouldn't be living underground. He didn't recognize me. I told him I was his daughter and I wasn't a ghost. He told me to call off my war and instead spend the next day swimming in the river where the water was like warm silk on skin. I told him that didn't make any sense.

It's me, Bianca, I said. I'm your daughter. Look at my face.

I rubbed the dirt from my cheeks. Made sure my face wasn't coated in snow or ash.

Bianca, I said. Don't you recognize me.

I wrote each letter of my name on a scrap of parchment and slid it across the floor.

B I A

N C A

My father moved the letters around. He spelled A CABIN. Then he came back to BIANCA. He looked at the letters, the name, then at me. He kept doing this.

Eventually I think he smiled.

Thaddeus

Something is wrong with me.

The Girl Who Smells of Honey and Smoke

I will help you and the town.

FEBRUARY GOES HOME. FEBRUARY
waited in the woods before heading home
to the girl who smelled of honey and
smoke. He opened the door and handed her
a sculpture of an owl with a cracked skull.
He bought it cheap from a depressed
sculptor. The girl who smelled of honey and
smoke cried and hugged February. She
whispered in his ear that Thaddeus Lowe
now believes in spring and that given time
it will infect the entire town.

Maybe we can live in peace, she said.

It was a solution to the war against him.
February had suffered through their fake
smiling faces, water-trough attacks, sticks
thrown at the sky, prayers and War
Hymns. He had seen them covered with
moss and endless layers of gray. He had
seen them saddened with over nine
hundred days of February, and he had
been blamed for it.

Very well, then, said February. And he
sat down in a wooden rocking chair and
folded his hands on his lap.

I love you, said the girl who smelled of
honey and smoke. And I love you, said
February, feeling a little sad.

Note Written by February

There is a house builder and his wife.
Name the house builder February and
refer to the wife as the girl who smells of
honey and smoke.

After Thaddeus called off all

wars against February, the town's sadness reached a new depth. Two members of the War Effort flung themselves from the blacksmith's ship. Another cut his wrists open in the middle of the street, and dead vines poured from his body, grew through the street and covered a cottage. Shopkeepers wept through the night. The beekeepers had their bees sting their necks in order to stop their crying. Snow mixed with ice and a sheet of lightning fell from the sky. And Thaddeus Lowe could be seen walking through town wearing nothing but cutoff burlap pants, commenting to his neighbors about the beautiful weather.

Remember to trim those hedges, he yelled to a shopkeeper who was sitting on a pile of dirty snow, his knees pulled up to his face as he rocked back and forth.

The underground children came up occasionally to watch the town fall apart. They thought of rebelling against Thaddeus on account of his madness. They held meetings and argued into the late night. They discussed the War Plan given to them by a girl who smelled of honey and smoke, seeing now the consequences of proceeding without the support of the War Effort and townsfolk. Their confusion swept through the underground tunnels.

Thaddeus dreamed and ignored everyone

in town telling him that February was still occurring. Squares of parchment tied with blue ribbon had been placed throughout his home. Each one had a different style of writing, each from a different person from town or the War Effort. They said things like how February had been the cause of his wife's death, his daughter's and Caldor Clemens's. They pleaded with Thaddeus to remember the days of flight, and one parchment had strands of balloon fabric sewn to the fibers. Thaddeus didn't touch any of these. It was Bianca who began sneaking into the home each evening, placing the squares of parchment around the house as her father drove a tractor through the imaginary fields. When he ignored them, she began unfolding the parchments and placing them in the bathtub, on his bed, sticking them inside cabinet doors with candle wax. Thaddeus started to read them and nailed them to the walls of his home until they covered each room. He studied what they said and thought that he should go back to the home of February in the woods and the girl who smells of honey and smoke and ask more questions.

The girl who smelled of honey and smoke

wanted to be with a man who had the following characteristics: (1) Gets his hair cut. (2) Has a respectable income. (3) Wears nice clothes that fit him. (4) Acts like a man. (5) Looks healthy. When she looked at February sitting on the floor, occasionally writing something, she saw none of this. His hair hadn't been cut in over six months. It was a mess of brown waves and curls, a dingy mat growing down the back of his neck that embarrassed her when she brought him around her friends. His job at a local store, where he had been working for over two years without a decent raise, was going nowhere. He didn't own a vehicle like other men,

because he couldn't afford one. Instead he rode his bike to work each day and didn't object when the girl who smelled of honey and smoke's parents offered to buy them a vehicle. He couldn't afford an apartment, so he lived in his parents' basement, where the girl who smelled of honey and smoke lived also and was now planning an escape each day she woke to the sound of someone's piss spraying the toilet water above her head. His wardrobe consisted of underwear his mother had bought him over six years ago when he first went away to college, a half dozen faded T-shirts and three pairs of jeans that were Christmas gifts from the past three years. When February would spend hours writing a story he wouldn't discuss because it had gotten away from him months before, the girl who smelled of honey and smoke told him that other men do things like take their girlfriends out, buy them flowers and candy, surprise them with picnics. A man, she said, doesn't hide some make-believe story that he can't even finish. And lastly, when she looked at February in the shower, or when he was dressing, she wondered if he was dying. His skin was pale, his arms and leg bones lacked the muscular frame that she believed was sexy. He was six foot two and weighed 155 pounds. Except for the two-mile bike ride to work, he decided against an exercise routine. Occasionally she'd see him in the bedroom, struggling on a third push-up, and she'd notice the uncombed block of hair, the tubelike body trembling, the dirty clothes piled up, the bicycle leaning against the drywall, and it reminded her of what she didn't have, the possibilities waiting outside those dark walls.

FEBRUARY HELD A BEARD TRIMMER.

He reread the list of characteristics the girl
who smelled of honey and smoke sought in
a man until the anger turned to sadness.
He stretched his arms out in front of him.
He inspected their thinness. He ran his
hands through his hair, the thickest part
at the back near his neck, a puffy mess
that now embarrassed even himself. Then,
flipping the plastic switch, that row of
rusty little teeth sawing back and forth,
February raised it to the front of his head
and in one long stroke began shaving off
his hair.

When the townsfolk looked up, they
believed that it was snowing but as the
locks of hair fell down upon their
shoulders, lashing them across their
cheeks, curling around their ankles and
holding them to the streets, sticking to
their lips and suffocating their breath, they
realized that it was another attack by
February.

Look, said Thaddeus to himself. Some
summer vines are falling from the clouds.
How unusual.

It's February, said a war member.

Thaddeus, please, it's February from above causing this. Can't you see that.

I'm going off to see February at the edge of town again, said Thaddeus.

Thaddeus, it's a trick. February doesn't live at the edge of town. Look up!

Thaddeus was off.

Thaddeus walked back through the

woods and to the home of February and the girl who smelled of honey and smoke. When he opened the door, he saw a man in a rocking chair cutting his hair with a pair of large sewing shears. The girl who smelled of honey and smoke was sitting on the floor writing on parchment paper, which she folded into tiny squares and bound with blue ribbon.

The man, thought Thaddeus, was February. He wore faded brown pants and a dark blue sweater with holes at the elbows. He cut his hair in odd angles and took a few snips from the chin of his beard.

Thaddeus closed the door.

February dropped the sewing shears. The girl pushed the parchment papers under a bearskin rug. They glanced at each other and looked back at Thaddeus, who was still standing in the doorway.

Well, come in, said February. Don't let the cold air in.

Thaddeus was puzzled. His ankles, beneath his socks, were sticky with sweat.

The girl who smelled of honey and smoke approached Thaddeus and placed her arms around his shoulders. I'm glad you're back, she said. Come in and sit on the floor with me.

February stayed in his rocking chair. He folded his hands in his lap and rocked back and forth. He looks scared, thought Thaddeus.

I thought you were dead, said Thaddeus, looking at February.

February shook his head no.

I'm not dead, he said. As a matter of fact, I don't know who or what I am anymore. Everyone in town is terrified of me. They blame me for an endless season where all it does is snow and the skies are gray and everyone is filled with endless sadness. They blame me for the end of flight. Did you know that I had visions that you were coming to cut my throat, Thaddeus. Just awful. I had to sleep in an empty cottage at the edge of another town. The weather was warm.

Thaddeus didn't know of any other town within walking distance.

February continued. I ran away from the possibility of you killing me to another town that appeared to be abandoned. The weather was warm, the homes newly built, but there were holes in the ground that appeared to go to the center of the earth. It looked like tunnels underground, and inside them were lamps strung like holiday lights.

The girl who smelled of honey and smoke got up to make tea. Thaddeus said yes, that he would drink tea only if the bottom of the cup were stuffed with mint leaves.

I don't understand, said Thaddeus to February.

Neither do we, said the girl who smelled of honey and smoke.

The two holes in the sky, February said, they hold

the answer. We believe in a Creator. We believe that the Creator is up inside those two holes in the sky. We believe that the cause of this endless sad season is directly connected to the Creator.

Thaddeus took the teacup from the girl who smelled of honey and smoke. But you're February, he said. You're the cause of it.

I'm not February, February said. You and everyone else including the Creator call me February. I don't even know my name. I'm a builder of houses, I know that. I built this house by myself. I should be called House Builder. Most of the homes in your town, I built with my bare hands. That is, before I was driven away. I hate February.

But you kidnapped the children and buried them, said Thaddeus.

I wouldn't do that, said House Builder, kind of laughing.

The girl who smelled of honey and smoke sat so close to Thaddeus on the floor that their knees were touching.

He loves children, she said. He wouldn't do that.

February the Creator kidnapped the children, said House Builder. February the Creator is responsible for this endless season of sadness.

But you, said Thaddeus, looking at the girl who smelled of honey and smoke. You poisoned me. You made me see spring. When my daughter was taken from her bed, it smelled of honey and smoke and the window was open.

Like I can control what I do and how you are affected. I believe I was only doing it for the safety of my husband. Someone told me to do it, and I did it. I, too, have been mislabeled as a girl who smells of honey and smoke. I'm a Housewife. And as for the smell of the room, Housewife whispered, February is a cruel being, capable of such tricks.

So it is still February, said Thaddeus. All this time February is still occurring.

I'm afraid so, she said.

None of this makes sense, thought Thaddeus.

We feel the same way, said House Builder.

How did you hear that.

You said it out loud, said House Builder. The girl who smelled of honey and smoke nodded.

There was a war planned by underground children, said Thaddeus. It's against February. Or is it against you. I shouldn't have called it off. Should I have called it off. I need to get back to town. And Thaddeus headed to the door.

Please, said House Builder. I know you won't understand this, because I believe it's impossible to understand, but I'm not the cause of the town's troubles. I've been pushed to the edge of town. Look back to the two holes in the sky. That's where the problem is. Or the problem is willpower and what you think you can control. I, for example, got labeled February and my wife here as a girl who smells of honey and smoke. Such nonsense. How awful.

When Thaddeus opened the door, it was snowing again and the trees were coated in ice. He ran back to the town as fast as he could, tripping and falling several times. He screamed in torment, his face pressed into the hard snow.

The girl who smelled of honey and smoke

woke up before February each morning. She'd crawl out of bed and walk through the darkness of the unfinished home and sit down at a wooden desk where she'd click on a small green lamp. She would read through the stacks of papers, the fragmented paragraphs, the half sentences and abandoned dialogue, and finish these lost riddles to her liking. A long time ago, she showed Bianca the sun. Yesterday she told Thaddeus to walk back to the house of a man wrongly accused of being February to ask more questions. She supplied the blacksmiths with the tools to build a ship. One by one she revived the children buried underground after February kidnapped them, and she was the one who dropped the scraps of parchment from the sky that Thaddeus and the War Effort collected. The girl who smelled of honey and smoke told the children nursery rhymes and supplied them with lanterns as her hands carved out the maze of tunnels. There, there, she said, hushing them to sleep under thick winter blankets, their bodies huddled against a curve in the tunnel. And deep inside their dreams, she fed them the images of a final War Plan against February. There, there, she whispered, tucking the squares of parchment under their pillowed heads.

Thaddeus called a meeting with the War Effort.

I apologize to everyone, he said. The past weeks I believed it was spring when in fact the attacks from February have never been worse. I believe we should go on a full-scale attack against February. He doesn't live at the edge of town. That is House Builder and his wife, who is a worker of spells and who tricked me to protect her husband. What I do know is that the real February is the Creator who lives in the two holes in the sky. We should have known this. We will immediately construct a fleet of balloons and ascend into the air.

There were about thirty people in Thaddeus's home, and they immediately began to object. A few people shouted that flight is impossible. The Professor quieted them and spoke.

But we already have a plan under way, he said, and handed Thaddeus the bundle of parchments gathered from the homes and shops left by the underground children.

Fine, go ahead with it, he said. But I'm going in the opposite direction. I need to get into the holes in the sky.

Should someone go with you, asked a war member.

No, said Thaddeus. The children's War Plan is a plan

that will work, but I can't leave without seeing what's in the sky. I will attempt to fly tomorrow by myself. Everyone else can begin the children's War Plan.

That night everyone ate dinner

together at the inn. They had steamed carrots, apple-glazed pork and boiled potatoes. They ate all the food in the town. They told stories of how New Town would be warmer. They drank and dreamed of blooming fields. A calendar was created, void of the season of February, and at the end of the night they brought it out and everyone cheered.

They talked over the War Plan one last time and went to bed early. People questioned Thaddeus on how he was going to fly when flight was impossible. Thaddeus shrugged his shoulders, said he didn't care, that he just had to try.

I miss you both, said Thaddeus that night into his pillow.

He thought about the man and the woman at the edge of town. His head was spinning.

I love you both, he said into the pillow.

And then he fell asleep.

FEBRUARY WOKE ONE MORNING AT THE
same time that the girl who smelled of
honey and smoke was getting up from the
bed. He decided to follow her. He crawled
on his hands and knees across the floor
and looked into the next room where the
desk was. The girl who smelled of honey
and smoke was sitting there writing
something. She was folding sheets of paper
and tying them with blue ribbon and
reaching her arm through a hole in the
floor. February stood up and walked to the
desk. The girl heard him. She turned
around.

Go ahead, he said, you can write
whatever you want, he said. I don't care
anymore.

I will, she said. You took away a man's
wife and daughter for no reason. You're
cruel. I'm going to show them happiness,
she said, wondering if he knew about the
underground children, the notes she had
given them.

I'm sorry, said February. I'm sorry for
everything.

February turned and walked back to the
bedroom. Just before he entered, a sharp
pain ran from the bottom of his foot to his

hip. He fell back on the ground and twisted his foot up near his chest. He saw three dead bees crushed into his heel.

Later that same day the

girl who smelled of honey and smoke sat at the desk and lit fires in the town. She had Bianca start at one house and work in a descending circle, burning it all down. She then collected the papers in a stack, tied it with ribbon, and placed it in a box she titled Light Box.

Bianca began at the edge

of town and worked in a descending circle, dipping and tilting her lantern into piles of brush that the War Effort had placed the day before the death of Caldor Clemens. On a parchment it looked like this:

The last home she set fire to before escaping down one of the tunnels was her own. When she ran inside, her chest hurt from breathing so hard and her blue dress was covered with ash. She looked out the window and saw the plains burning and the blacksmith ship sailing away in the distance. She walked around the house, lighting the walls with a growing flame as the children and townsfolk yelled beneath her.

Come on, Bianca, they said. Come now before you burn to death. Their fists pounded the soles of her feet.

She slid a floorboard to the side and saw all their dirty little faces underneath.

In you go now, said one of the smallest children from deep below.

As she climbed down she thought she heard her father scream her name.

Six Reports from the Priests

1. We can see Bianca in the distance.

2. She runs from brush pile to brush pile dipping her lantern and sparking flames that are spreading throughout the town.

3. She's wearing a blue dress and yellow socks, and drawings of kites on her hands and arms glow in the light of the fire. She is a streak of color with long black hair.

4. There are seven of us here in the woods. We have no place to go without the direction of our Creator and with the fire reaching the first line of birch trees. We fear for our lives.

5. The snow turns to pools of water around our toes. There's a loud creaking sound that echoes through the woods.

6. The last thing we see is the blacksmith ship moving through the town. It divides shops in two. Splinters of flaming wood spin through the air.

The Girl Who Smelled of Honey and Smoke

I write in huge letters

FLIGHT RETURNED
TO TOWN

and fold it into a little square and go back to bed with February.

When I wake in the middle of the night, I have an idea. I make a drawing of a New Town on parchment, and that, too, I fold into a little square.

In the morning I take the folded squares and place them under the pillow of Thaddeus Lowe. Thaddeus repeats out loud the sentence FLIGHT RETURNED TO TOWN and smiles.

Thaddeus wore the light box

on his head when he ascended in the balloon toward the holes in the sky. Beneath him the town was flames and dark smoke. It filled the sky around him. From a great distance, where the rest of the town was climbing up from the tunnels and into their new homes, they could see the balloon glowing with each pulse of flame and a box of light flickering in the darkness.

What's going to happen to him, said one of the children.

Maybe he's going to die, said another, throwing a large burlap sack of clothing onto the ground.

He's not going to die, said another child. He's going to be with the Creator.

Bianca was in her new home. She watched out the window the old town in the distance burn to the ground. She saw the balloon light and disappear, and she played the ancient game of Prediction. She saw a box of light sitting on the shoulders of her shouting father. The kites on her hands and arms burned. She wanted to throw the kites out from her fingers and into the sky and tie them to the balloon and pull her father back to earth. She saw the balloon ascend to the two holes in the sky. She saw the balloon stop.

The top of the balloon

was stuck. Thaddeus climbed out of the basket and up the side of the balloon. He had draped thick ropes there for this purpose. When he came to the edge of the hole in the sky, he pulled himself up and kicked against the balloon. He crawled on his stomach until he was completely inside a large room that looked just like House Builder's home. It was dark except for a small lamp that sat on a desk. The room smelled like honey and smoke, and Thaddeus walked around a little before hearing footsteps and hiding behind the furniture. It was the girl who smelled of honey and smoke. She carried a steaming cup. She sat down at the desk and began to write. All around the desk were little squares of paper tied with blue ribbon.

Hello, whispered Thaddeus, peeking over a piece of furniture.

The girl who smelled of honey and smoke didn't hear him.

It's me, he whispered a little louder.

The girl who smelled of honey and smoke turned around.

You, she said. Go away. What are you doing here. I'm trying to save you from February.

I know what's going on, said Thaddeus. I know that February lives here and he is a mean man who named House Builder and his wife February and the girl who smelled of honey and smoke.

She looked at him. He's not a mean man, she said. He's just confused. He didn't know what to do with your town. But I'm helping now. It's over. February has given up. I'm giving you a New Town and a new life. You really should go.

How big is our town, Thaddeus asked, looking back through the hole in the floor, the sky of the town.

I have no idea, said the girl who smelled of honey and smoke. I mean it when I say you should go back. Everything is going to be fine now.

Is February here.

Yes, but he's sleeping.

Thaddeus said, I want to see February.

No, you can't. There's no point in it.

I want to see February, said Thaddeus.

Fine, said the girl. But very quickly.

The girl who smelled of honey and smoke led Thaddeus into a cold bedroom. A man was sleeping under the sheets. His hair was brown and curly. He looked sad.

That's him. That's February.

Yes, said the girl. Are you happy now.

I hate him, said Thaddeus. I hate him for what he did.

Thaddeus stood. His chest rose and fell. He felt the sharp tip of the knife in his pocket.

The Girl Who Smells of Honey and Smoke Creates New Town

After the smoke cleared from the skies, the sun came out big and glorious and the leaves on the trees looked like they were on fire. Crop fields and flower beds bloomed. Some of the children went blind from staring in disbelief at the sun. They had to walk around with cloth tied around their eyes. Bianca told everyone that the sun possessed this power, but even she stared at it and now saw black spots in the corners of the new sky.

Scraps of Parchment Written by the Girl Who Smells of Honey and Smoke

Everyone smiled in New Town.

No one mentioned the old town ever again.

The season of February existed only in the old town.

Caldor Clemens unhanged himself from deep in the woods and came to New Town. He walked into a shop and asked, Did I miss anything, and everyone laughed.

Selah, frozen in the river, was seen one morning crawling from the muddy shore. She remembered nothing.

February at the edge of town and his wife came to New Town and explained how his name was House Builder and not February. He told the story of February the Creator and his war with not only the town but with a girl who smelled of honey and smoke.

Only Thaddeus Lowe was missing.

February

I hear a man breathing. I hear the girl who smells of honey and smoke say,

put down the knife.

Thaddeus

The girl who smelled of honey and smoke told me to hide. So I did. I watched from behind a curtain as February got up from his bed. He was a skinny man. He didn't look scary. He said something to the girl who smelled of honey and smoke about hearing her talking to someone. A man. She denied it. He asked where the light box was, and she said that she thought he was finished with it.

February said, No, I'm not. I don't think I am after all.

The girl who smelled of honey and smoke handed him a box. February uncovered it and took out a stack of parchment.

New Town, he said. What is this.

I heard a dog, no, a wolf, howling. Then I saw February run from the room with the stack of parchment. I heard heavy footsteps near the top of my head. Where was I.

FEBRUARY UPSTAIRS SCRIBBLES THADDEUS
Lowe drowns. Thaddeus Lowe is attacked
by bears. Thaddeus Lowe has a heart
attack. Thaddeus Lowe chokes to death on
an apple. Thaddeus Lowe's mouth fills with
snow.

Downstairs, the girl who smells

of honey and smoke writes, Thaddeus Lowe becomes a famous balloonist. Thaddeus Lowe has three more children and becomes New Town mayor. Thaddeus Lowe lives to be a hundred years old. Thaddeus Lowe forgets the definition of sadness.

She hears a bear growling in the closet where Thaddeus is. She hears Thaddeus say his heart hurts. She hears Thaddeus say he is having a wonderful life, but the closet is filling with water and he doesn't know how to swim and his mouth is filling with snow and he's choking.

FEBRUARY FLIPS THROUGH THE STACK
of parchment and finds a single sheet
that says, THADDEUS WORE THE
LIGHT BOX ON HIS HEAD WHEN HE
ASCENDED IN THE BALLOON
TOWARD THE TWO HOLES IN THE
SKY.

February didn't remember writing that.
He ran back downstairs and searched the
room.

Is he actually here, he asked the girl who
smelled of honey and smoke. Is it actually
possible that Thaddeus is here.

The girl who smelled of honey and smoke
said nothing. She stood with her hands
behind her back, a pencil in one hand,
parchment in the other. She had grown to
resent him for what he had done to the
town. She had loved him. She had hated
him. February looked at the closet, the
slight wavering of the fabric.

Thaddeus trembled. He had his knife
drawn. February reached his hand out and
pulled the curtain to the side and felt a
blade sink into his chest, stopping at the
bone. Thaddeus pushed February across
the room. The two spun in circles before
falling to the floor. The town looked up and

saw the sky shake. February hit Thaddeus on the side of the face with a closed fist. A tooth fell from the sky. The knife sank deeper, twisted to the left, then the right. The girl who smelled of honey and smoke screamed, STOP, STOP. She tried to separate them, pulling at flailing arms and legs. February bit Thaddeus's ear and drew blood. Thaddeus took the knife out and drove it down, hard, at the shoulder. Then into his stomach, where he zigzagged a deep path. He kept stabbing February, sinking the blade in deeper and faster with each hit. Blood soaked February—a lake growing from his chest. His hands waved near Thaddeus's face, pulling at his mouth and poking his eyes. February screamed, coughed up blood and a white flower petal, and then the resistance of his body loosened. When the town looked up, they saw bloodred vines twist through the sky. Giant flowers bloomed over clouds. The vines and flowers grew in layers until they reached the outstretched fingertips.

Note Found in February's Pocket by the Girl Who Smells of Honey and Smoke

I wanted to write you a story about magic. I wanted rabbits appearing from hats. I wanted balloons lifting you into the sky. It turned out to be nothing but sadness, war, heartbreak. You never saw it, but there's a garden inside me.

Thaddeus moved from the body

of February and leaped through the hole and back into the balloon. He heard the girl who smelled of honey and smoke crying. He looked at the blood that covered his hands and arms. He trembled. The balloon descended into the town of flowers, bumping, getting caught several times on the vine growth. When the balloon reached the ground everyone was cheering. It was a New Town. Thaddeus didn't smile or cheer. He simply looked back up at the two holes in the sky and waited for something to happen.

He waited.

The girl who smelled of honey and smoke

sat on the floor with the body of February. She kissed him on his forehead. When she rolled him over to see the two holes in the floor she saw vines and flowers and blood growing from his back. She didn't feel anger against Thaddeus or regret. She didn't feel anything. She wrote June on one sheet of parchment and July on the other and then colored them yellow. Then she crumpled up the two sheets of parchment and stuffed one in one hole and one in the other. Then she went upstairs and grabbed a large rug. She carried the rug downstairs, and she unfolded it and placed it over the floor and the two holes in the sky.

Thaddeus

We look at the
sky for hours.
There are two suns
in the sky. One sun
has June written
on it and the other
sun says July.

The Professor makes a calendar with these two seasons. The vines and flowers from the sky cover the ground. The flowers are the size of our heads. The children kick them around. The crop fields stretch toward the sky. It's so hot. My feet sink into the warm mud. The idea of February becomes erased from our thoughts. The Solution begins construction on new balloons. A baby is crying. More than one baby is crying. Dozens of naked babies with flowers wrapped around their throats are walking from the horizon toward us. They scream, and huge white flowers unfold from their little mouths and float like balloons up into the sky.

End

End

End

End

End

End

End

End

End

End

End

End

End

End

End

End

End

End

End

End

End

End

End

End

End

End

End

END